GIGANTOSAURUS ™

Rock Out, ROCKY

templar
books

A TEMPLAR BOOK

This book is based on the episode *Rock Out* from the TV series *Gigantosaurus* ™.
Screenplay by Maria O'Loughlin & Jacqui Moody.
The TV series *Gigantosaurus* ™ is created and produced by Cyber Group Studios.
Based on the original characters created by Jonny Duddle in the book *Gigantosaurus*,
first published by Templar Books in 2014.

First published in the UK by Templar Books, an imprint of Bonnier Books UK
The Plaza, 535 King's Road, London SW10 0SZ
Owned by Bonnier Books, Sveavägen 56, Stockholm, Sweden

© 2020 Cyber Group Studios

1 3 5 7 9 10 8 6 4 2

ISBN 978-1-78741-599-7

Adapted by Harriet Paul & Dynamo Ltd.
Edited by Lydia Watson & Carly Blake
Designed by Dynamo Ltd.
Additional design by Adam Allori
Production Controller: Ché Creasey

Printed in China

Rocky has hidden **10** of his
favourite Giganto cards
throughout this book.

Can you find them all?

This story is all about **ROCKY**, the plucky parasaurolophus. He's the fastest, strongest and TOUGHEST dino in the whole Cretaceous world . . . or so he thinks! Here's how Rocky learned that everyone needs a little help from their friends sometimes – even the toughest dinosaur of all!

It was a sunny day in Cretacia and Rocky had challenged himself to complete another daring mission.

This time, he was running as fast as his legs would carry him, up the fiery path of the biggest volcano in the land – MOUNT OBLIVION!

"How am I doing?" Rocky called to his friends.

Mazu was timing him on her sundial rock. "You're set to break the record!" she shouted.

Fastest dino to reach the top of Mount Oblivion!

Halfway up the mountain, Rocky paused to deliver one of his typical 'tough guy' speeches to his friends.

"That's me – ROCKY. The TOUGHEST, FASTEST volcano climber in all the land. Soon every dinosaur will know who I am."

Even GIGANTOSAURUS!

Mazu, Bill and Tiny had heard this speech a hundred times before.

"He's daydreaming about his hero again," they laughed.

As Rocky stepped back, he tripped over a small rock and sent it flying. Although he was a very daring dinosaur, he could also be VERY clumsy.

The small rock bumped into a HUGE boulder, which went rolling down the volcano at speed – straight towards his friends!

Luckily the boulder missed the other dinos by a fraction . . . but poor Rocky had hurt his foot on the rock. His friends rushed over to take care of him.

"Here, let us help you!" said Tiny.

"Help? NO WAY," scoffed Rocky. "Tough dinos like Giganto walk alone!"

"ALONE?" the others gasped.

I think he's hurt!

Are you OK, Rocky?

Rocky pulled out his trusty Giganto cards and held them up one by one to prove his point.

"See – here he is jogging . . . ALONE.

And here he is in a mud bath built for ONE!"

"And my personal favourite – here's Giganto food shopping. Also carried out ALONE. So, I too have to prove how tough I am. ALONE!" Rocky finished dramatically.

Rocky's friends sighed. How would Rocky make it to the top of the volcano with an injured foot if he wouldn't let them help?

Suddenly, the ground underneath the dinos SHOOK with a mighty RUMBLE. It was a GROUNDWOBBLER!

The cliff the little dinosaurs were standing on broke away from the mountain with a CRACK and took them sailing down the river of lava at full speed! At the base of the volcano they slid to a sudden stop and Rocky soared through the air . . .

WOAAAHHHH!

. . . before landing neatly in Tiny's arms.

Gotcha, tough guy!

"Ugh, Tiny, why did you have to help me?" Rocky said grumpily. "I told you, I don't need ANYONE'S help!"

The four friends had landed just outside the jungle. The noise from the groundwobbler was coming from within and it was getting LOUDER! A stampede of creatures thundered past, rushing to get away from the earth-shaking sound.

That gave Rocky an idea.

"I'm going to check it out," he said. "If I can't break the record to the top of Mount Oblivion, then I'll stop the earth from wobbling instead!"

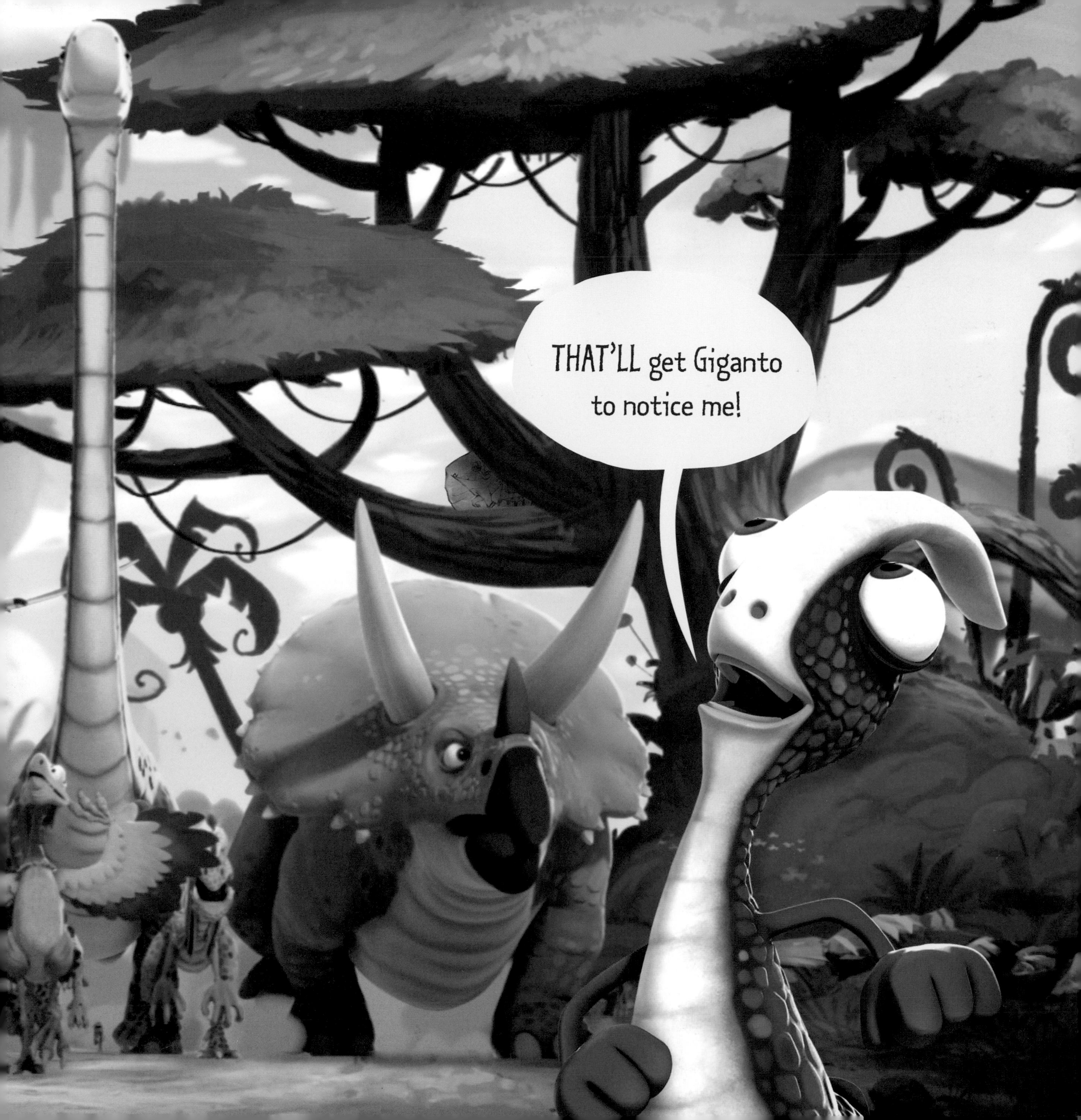
THAT'LL get Giganto to notice me!

"Is your crest filled with coconuts?!" asked Bill in disbelief. "You don't run TOWARDS danger – you run AWAY from it!"

"Not this parasora . . . parasloppa . . . SUPER DINO!" said Rocky, heading off towards where the rumbling sound was coming from.

"I think he meant 'parasaurolophus'!" said Mazu.

Rocky was happy to be back on his tough guy mission. As he walked along, he was busy thinking up a tough-sounding new nickname for himself. "It needs to be something super-cool, like . . . GIGANTO," he thought.

Rockinator? Rockster?
ROCK-A-DOODLE-DOO?

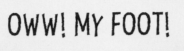

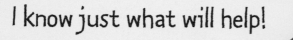

I know just what will help!

The others heard Rocky shout out in pain and hurried along to help. His foot was still hurting badly. Mazu looked around and spotted a pink plant nearby.

"This is a bulb from a java plant!" she said excitedly. "It's full of gel that will help your foot feel better."

"I don't NEED your help!" Rocky said angrily. He was still annoyed with his friends.

"Everybody needs help sometimes," said Mazu, feeling hurt.

But Rocky wouldn't listen. "Not tough guys like . . ."

... GIGANTOSAURUS!

"Wow!" Rocky gazed up at his idol with wonder.

Suddenly, the mighty dinosaur started to hop UP and DOWN on one foot and the ground began to RUMBLE and SHAKE. So Giganto was the groundwobbler! But why was he stomping around so much?

Then Mazu spotted something in Giganto's foot. "Isn't that the boulder Rocky knocked over earlier?" she asked. Sure enough, the same rock was now wedged between Giganto's toes.

Poor Giganto! He's hurt!

"I bet if we calm him down, we could get that rock out from between his toes," said Tiny.

Rocky sprang into action. It was his fault, so he thought he should be the one to fix it! How could he calm Giganto down? "I've got it!" he said excitedly. "When I was a baby, my mum would MOO to help me relax."

Rocky took a deep breath and blew air
out of the crest on his head. It made
a deep MOOOOOOO sound that echoed
through the jungle. Giganto stopped
stomping and tilted his head down
to listen.

"I think it's working!" said Mazu.

MOOOOOOOO

"I've got to get closer!" said Rocky, determined.
He scrambled over to a palm tree and started to climb up.

But he soon slipped and fell back down to the ground with a CRASH!
Rocky wasn't going anywhere with his sore foot.

Mazu squirted the java plant gel onto Rocky's foot and he instantly felt better. "See how nice a little help can be?" she said.

"I'm sorry," said Rocky, looking up at his friends. "I should have just accepted your help in the first place."

Then the ground shook again, and Rocky remembered his mission.

"Giganto!" he cried. "Now it's HIS turn to feel better. I'm coming, big guy! I mean . . . WE'RE coming."

With his foot feeling much better, Rocky hopped up onto a tree branch and blew air out of his crest to relax the huge dinosaur. Meanwhile, Mazu and Tiny used a bamboo stick to pry the rock out from between Giganto's toes. Finally, Bill spread java gel onto his foot to make it feel better.

The four dino friends cheered as Giganto stomped off.
He was looking much happier.

"Rocky, you did it!" said Tiny. "You made Giganto better!"

"No," smiled Rocky. "WE did it. I couldn't have done it without you!"

That was how Rocky learned that sometimes the toughest thing a dinosaur can do is accept help from his friends – even when he thinks he doesn't need it! Rocky became a much more humble dinosaur after that . . . well, for a few minutes at least!

Wait . . . this book is all about ME?!

I'M FAMOUS!

Here he goes again!